MOON PLANE

written and illustrated by

PETER M^CCARTY

Henry Holt and Company

New York

Henry Holt and Company, LLC

Publishers since 1866

175 Fifth Avenue, New York, New York 10010

www.henryholtchildrensbooks.com

Distributed in Canada by H. B. Fenn and Company Ltd.

Library of Congress Cataloging-in-Publication Data

McCarty, Peter.

Moon plane / Peter McCarty.— 1st ed.

p.   cm.

Summary: A young boy looks at a plane in the sky and

imagines flying one all the way to the moon.

ISBN-13: 978-0-8050-7943-2

ISBN-10: 0-8050-7943-2

[1. Airplanes—Fiction. 2. Flight—Fiction. 3. Moon—Fiction.] I. Title.

PZ7.M478403Moo 2006   [E]—dc22   2005016244

First Edition—2006 / Designed by Donna Mark

The artist used pencil on watercolor paper

to create the illustrations for this book.

Printed in China on acid-free paper. ∞

1 3 5 7 9 10 8 6 4 2

For my sisters,

Annie and Mary Ellen

Above the clouds
an airplane flies
into the sky.

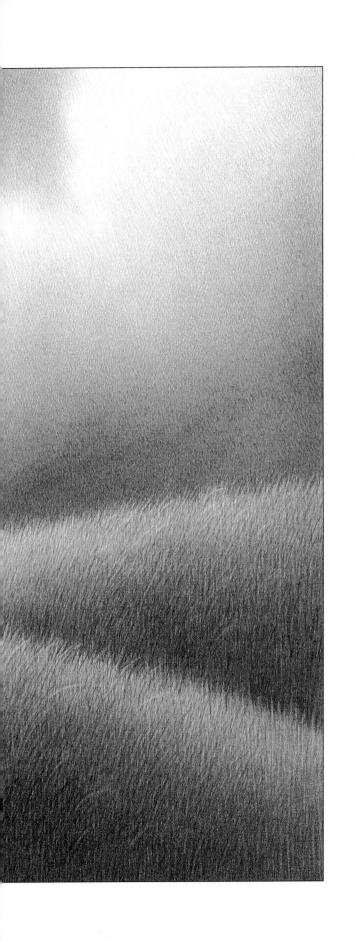

On the ground
a small boy
looks up.

He wonders
what it would be like
to be on that flight.

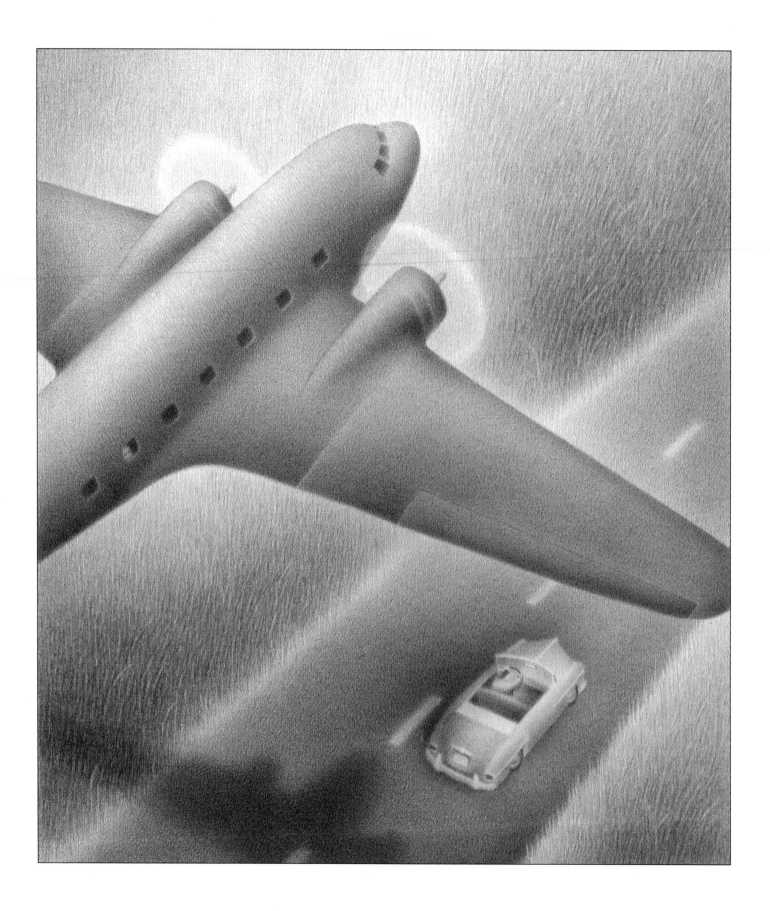

To glide over a car
rolling down the road.

To soar past a train
speeding down the tracks.

To travel farther than a boat
sailing on the ocean.

If the small boy
were on that airplane,
he and that airplane
would fly into
outer space.

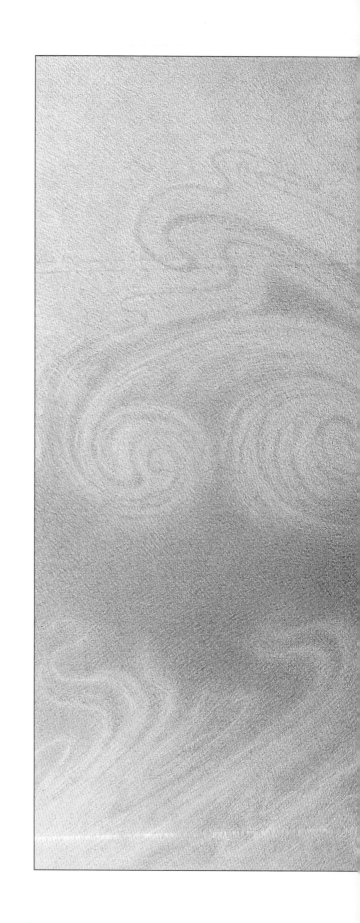

They would fly
all the way to the moon
where the airplane
would gently land.

On the surface of the moon
the small boy would take
a few steps,
jump...

. . . and fly
just like the airplane.

But soon,
the small boy
would have to return.

Back to the earth.

Back to the house.

Back to his mother
who would be waiting for him.

For that small boy,
who would go to bed
and dream of airplanes
flying high into the sky.

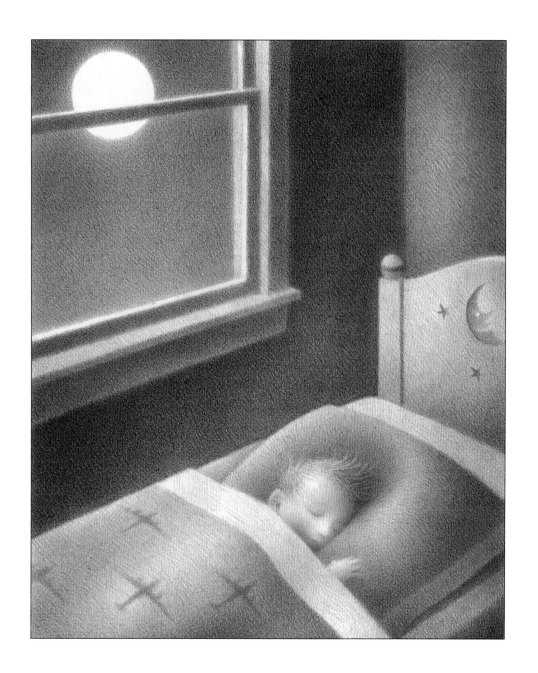